Flatfoot Fox

and the Case of the Missing Whoooo

Flatfoot Fox

and the Case of the Missing Whoooo

ETH CLIFFORD

Illustrated by Brian Lies

Scholastic Inc.

New York   Toronto   London
Auckland   Sydney

For Ed and Mim, Martin and Adrienne,
with love — E. C.

For Sam and Jane Keith
— B. L.

ISBN 0-590-48483-4

12 11 10 9 8 7 6 5 4 3   6 7 8 9/9

Printed in the U.S.A.   09

First Scholastic printing, September 1994

Contents

1
Silly Goose

Flatfoot Fox, the greatest detective in the whole world, had just opened his front door. He was almost knocked over by a breathless visitor.

"A terrible thing has happened," the visitor cried.

"Who are you?" asked Secretary Bird.

"Never mind that," Flatfoot Fox snapped. "What terrible thing has happened?"

"I am Silly Goose," said the visitor. He took a deep breath. "We need a detective. We need a detective in a hurry."

Flatfoot Fox nodded. "You have come to the right place," he said. "What is wrong? Why do you need a detective?"

Silly Goose took another deep breath. "Someone has stolen Mournful Owl's *whoooo*."

"His what?" Flatfoot Fox asked with surprise.

"No, no, no. Not his what. His *whoooo*," said Silly Goose."

Flatfoot Fox was puzzled. "How can anyone steal a who?"

"I don't know," Silly Goose answered. "That's why we need you."

"Yes, you certainly do need me," Flatfoot Fox agreed. "But first, tell me what you know about all this."

"And start at the beginning," Secretary Bird said.

"Last night," said Silly Goose, "Mournful Owl had his *whoooo*. He had it all night long. Then he went to sleep. When he woke up, his *whoooo* was gone."

"Who was there when Mournful Owl woke up?" Flatfoot Fox wanted to know.

"His *whoooo* wasn't there. I just told you that."

8

Flatfoot Fox sighed. "I mean, was anyone else there when Mournful Owl woke up?"

"Only me. No one else."

"No one? Are you sure?"

"No one. Now Mournful Owl just sits on a branch and stares straight ahead with sad eyes."

"So then Mournful Owl asked you to come and get me?" Flatfoot Fox asked.

Silly Goose shook his head. "No. He can't do anything but cry. I had to do something . . ."

"And that was when you decided to come to me for help," Flatfoot Fox said.

Secretary Bird nodded. "Now that was sensible," he said. "Very sensible."

Silly Goose was proud of himself. "I made up some posters, too. I brought one to show you," he told Flatfoot Fox.

Silly Goose held up his poster. The words were printed in large letters.

LOST OR STOLEN. A *WHOOOO*.
BIG REWARD FOR ITS RETURN.
NO QUESTIONS ASKED.

"What kind of reward?" asked Secretary Bird. Maybe, he thought, he could find the *whoooo* first. Then he would get the reward and wouldn't have to share it.

"A great big goose egg, of course," said Silly Goose.

Flatfoot Fox laughed, but Secretary Bird was angry. "What kind of a reward is that? Who would want a goose egg?"

"Another goose?" asked Silly Goose.

"A goose egg is a great big nothing. A zero. You silly goose," Secretary Bird shouted, "we refuse to take this case."

Flatfoot Fox shook his head. "You're wrong," he said. "I will take this case. I have never had one like this before."

Secretary Bird sighed.

Flatfoot Fox, it was easy to see, was eager to solve Mournful Owl's problem. Now he wouldn't rest until he solved it.

Flatfoot Fox had what he wanted — a new case that was a true mystery.

2
Early Bird Robin and
Cranky Worm

Flatfoot Fox and Secretary Bird went out the front door. Silly Goose followed them.

"Where are we going?" he asked.

"I am going to keep my eyes open, listen very hard, and ask questions," said Flatfoot Fox.

"Oh," said Silly Goose. "I see."

But he didn't see at all. Why was Flatfoot Fox going to keep his eyes open? Did he usually close them when he was detecting? And what was he going to listen for?

"Are you detecting now?" Silly Goose asked as he rushed to keep up with Flatfoot Fox.

"Shhhh!" said Flatfoot Fox. "I hear something."

What he heard was Early Bird Robin talking to

Cranky Worm. When Early Bird Robin saw them, he scolded Flatfoot Fox. "Look what you've done, you and your parade. You made me lose my worm."

"I am not your worm. I am not anybody's worm," said Cranky Worm.

"Don't be ridiculous. Of course you're my worm," Early Bird Robin told him. "Don't you know that the early bird catches the worm?" He turned to Flatfoot Fox. "Go on. Tell him. Doesn't the early bird catch the worm?"

"That's what I've heard," Flatfoot Fox agreed.

"See?" said Early Bird Robin. "Why don't we just get on with it? Why can't you be a nice little worm and let me eat you? I haven't had breakfast yet, and I am terribly hungry."

"I don't want to be your breakfast," said Cranky Worm.

"Breakfast can wait," said Flatfoot Fox. "I need to ask some questions."

"Before breakfast?" Early Bird Robin was surprised. "Nobody asks questions before breakfast."
16

"I do," said Flatfoot Fox, "so listen carefully. Something terrible has happened. Someone has stolen Mournful Owl's *whoooo*. Do you know anything about that?"

"Don't look at me," said Cranky Worm. "Mournful Owl should be more careful and not leave a *whoooo* around where anyone could steal it."

"Cranky Worm is right," said Early Bird Robin. "What good is a *whoooo*, anyway? You can't eat it, can you?"

"Were you anywhere near Mournful Owl this morning?" Flatfoot Fox asked Early Bird Robin. "Did you see or hear anything unusual?"

"I didn't know I was supposed to," said Early Bird Robin. "Wait," he shouted as Cranky Worm slid underground. But Cranky Worm refused to come up again.

"Now see what you've done," Early Bird Robin scolded. "You and your missing *whoooo*s." And he flew away.

Silly Goose was disappointed. "Are you sure

you're the greatest detective in the whole world?"
he asked Flatfoot Fox.

Secretary Bird nipped him. "You think you can
solve this case?"

When Silly Goose shook his head, Secretary Bird
went on: "Then be quiet and let Flatfoot Fox work
on this case his own way."

Flatfoot Fox paid no attention to them. He was
busy thinking. He asked himself two important
questions: how could someone have stolen Mournful Owl's *whoooo,* and why would anyone want to
steal it?

3
Pushy Peacock

Flatfoot Fox did his best thinking when he walked. He moved away so quickly, Secretary Bird and Silly Goose had to run to catch up with him.

They all moved so fast, they almost ran into a large bird standing in their way.

It was Pushy Peacock.

"Who are you? And what do you want? Speak up," Pushy Peacock said. "I haven't got all day, you know."

Silly Goose was surprised. "You mean you don't know who this is? This is Flatfoot Fox, the smartest detective in the whole world."

"Then why isn't he detecting?" Pushy Peacock asked.

"That's just what I'm doing," Flatfoot Fox told him. "Mournful Owl has lost his *whoooo*. It was probably stolen. I am working on the case."

"I should be the one to work on this case," Pushy Peacock said. "I would be a much better detective."

"Why is that?" Flatfoot Fox wanted to know.

"Watch," said Pushy Peacock.

As they watched, Pushy Peacock spread his wings and train wide open.

"See?" said Pushy Peacock. "I have a hundred eyes. And three extra eyes on the top of my head. If something is missing, who could see it better or faster than I?"

Before Flatfoot Fox could speak, Silly Goose said, "You're right. I should have come to you. A hundred eyes! And three more on the top of your head."

Even Secretary Bird was surprised. Maybe Silly Goose wasn't so silly after all.

"Maybe you can work with Pushy Peacock," Secretary Bird told Flatfoot Fox. "After all, two heads are better than one."

"Two heads?" asked Silly Goose. "I've never seen anyone with two heads. How would it work? Which head would do the talking? Which head would do the thinking?"

"No, no, no," said Secretary Bird. "What a silly goose you are. You must have sawdust for brains. I just meant that Flatfoot Fox and Pushy Peacock could work together as a team."

"No," said Flatfoot Fox. "The smartest detective in the world doesn't need help from anyone. I solve my cases by myself." He turned to stare at Pushy Peacock. "You say you want to be a detective. How would you go about finding Mournful Owl's missing *whoooo?*"

"How?" Pushy Peacock laughed. "Watch this." He spread his wings and train again. "I would use my hundred eyes, of course. And the three extra eyes on my head."

"And that would help you find the missing *whoooo?*" asked Flatfoot Fox.

"Of course," said Pushy Peacock.

"Tell me," said Flatfoot Fox. "How do you *see* a *whoooo?*"

Pushy Peacock stared at Flatfoot Fox. "What? What did you say?"

24

"How do you *see* a *whoooo?*" Flatfoot Fox asked again.

"Oh," said Silly Goose.

"Oh," said Secretary Bird.

"Oh," said Pushy Peacock.

"Think about it," Flatfoot Fox said, and walked away.

Silly Goose and Secretary Bird rushed after him.

"Wait, wait," Silly Goose called. When he caught up with Flatfoot Fox, he asked, "Are you still on the case?"

"Of course I'm still on the case," Flatfoot Fox told him. "When I'm on a case, I never give up. Never."

Flatfoot Fox hurried on.

Silly Goose and Secretary Bird had to run to keep up with him.

Then, suddenly, Flatfoot Fox stopped walking. He stood very still.

"What's he doing now?" asked Silly Goose.

"He's looking up into that tree."

"Why?" asked Silly Goose.

They were soon to find out.

4
What's a Thatsit?

"What is it? What do you see?" Secretary Bird asked.

He couldn't see anything.

Silly Goose couldn't see anything.

Flatfoot Fox didn't answer. He just stood very still. He looked and he listened. He listened and he looked.

Silly Goose whispered, "I wish I had Pushy Peacock's hundred eyes. And the three extra eyes on his head. Then I could see something, too."

"Be still," Secretary Bird whispered. "Flatfoot Fox's brain is working hard."

"Does it hurt?" asked Silly Goose. He was sure that if he had a brain, and used it, it would hurt a lot.

They waited and waited. It seemed like a long time, but it was only a minute or maybe two minutes.

Then Flatfoot Fox shouted, "That's it! That's it!"

"What's a thatsit?" Silly Goose wondered. "Is it a new kind of frog? It must be," he answered himself. "Because that's what I hear up in that tree. A frog."

"You don't hear a frog," Secretary Bird said. "You hear a bird. There's a woodpecker up in that tree."

"Exactly," said Flatfoot Fox. "I have solved the case."

Secretary Bird stared at Flatfoot Fox.

Silly Goose stared at Flatfoot Fox.

"I see," said Silly Goose, who didn't see at all. "A woodpecker who sounds like a frog is a thatsit. And a thatsit steals *whoooo*s."

Silly Goose was very proud of himself. It wasn't

hard to solve a case, after all. He didn't have a brain, but he could solve a case. Why, he hadn't needed Flatfoot Fox at all.

"You stole Mournful Owl's *whoooo*," Silly Goose shouted up at the thatsit. "You give it back. Right now."

Secretary Bird was disappointed. That's what he told Flatfoot Fox: "I'm disappointed. I thought it would take a long time to solve this case. Now it's been solved. The woodpecker stole the *whoooo*."

Flatfoot Fox shook his head. "No, he is not the thief."

The thatsit was not the thief?

Silly Goose was surprised.

So was Secretary Bird. "But you said 'That's it,' and you said you solved the case."

"So I did, and so I have," said Flatfoot Fox.

"But how did you do it?" asked Secretary Bird.

"The woodpecker gave me the clue," said Flatfoot Fox. He saw how puzzled Silly Goose looked. "A clue," he explained, "is something that helps you solve a mystery."

Silly Goose said, "Oh."

So a woodpecker who sounded like a frog and was called a thatsit gave clues that solved a mystery.

Silly Goose didn't have a brain, but his head hurt a lot anyway. From now on, he would leave all the thinking to Flatfoot Fox.

"Come along," said Flatfoot Fox. He sounded very pleased.

Secretary Bird knew that when Flatfoot Fox sounded pleased, his job was almost over.

Mournful Owl would get back his *whoooo*.

5

Who Stole the *Whoooo?*

"Come along, come along," Flatfoot Fox shouted, and ran on ahead.

"Where are we going?" asked Silly Goose. "Why is he always in such a hurry? Rush, rush, rush. And we still don't know who stole the *whoooo*."

"Flatfoot Fox knows. That's why he is in a hurry. He wants to catch the thief."

Silly Goose shook his head. "Like Early Bird Robin wanted to catch Cranky Worm? But Cranky Worm got away. Maybe the thief will get away, too."

"Nobody gets away from Flatfoot Fox," Secretary Bird said.

"Not ever?"

"Never," said Secretary Bird, and ran after Flat-foot Fox.

When Silly Goose caught up with them, Flatfoot Fox was staring up at a tree.

Secretary Bird was staring, too.

"What are you looking at?" asked Silly Goose. "Who's up there?"

Just then he heard a sound. A cat was mewing. Mew, mew, mew.

"Oh," said Silly Goose. "A cat is in the tree and can't get down. Poor little thing."

"Shhh," said Secretary Bird.

"It's not a cat," said Flatfoot Fox. "It's a catbird."

"A *bird?* That makes sounds like a cat?" Silly Goose shook his head.

It was all too much for him. First they met a bird that sounded like a frog. Now there was a bird that sounded like a cat.

Why couldn't a bird just sound like a bird? Silly Goose always sounded just like a goose.

"Hello up there," Flatfoot Fox shouted suddenly.

"I want to talk to you."

"I don't have time. I'm too busy," the catbird called back. "Who are you?"

"I am Flatfoot Fox."

"The smartest detective in the whole world," Secretary Bird said.

"I don't need a detective," said the catbird. "Go away."

"No. Mournful Owl needs a detective," Flatfoot Fox said. "Come down, Copycat."

"Copycat? Copycat Catbird?" Silly Goose asked in surprise.

Flatfoot Fox nodded.

"Why do you call him that?" asked Silly Goose.

"He is a copycat," Secretary Bird said. "He imitates other birds. He even imitates other animals. Like the cat."

Copycat Catbird hopped down to a low branch.

"You stole Mournful Owl's *whoooo*," said Flatfoot Fox.

"I did not," said Copycat Catbird. "I didn't steal it. I just borrowed it. For practice. So I would get the sound right. You have no idea how hard it is."

"Then why did you do it?" asked Silly Goose. "I never do anything hard if I can help it."

"I have to," Copycat Catbird explained. "Because that's what I am, a copycat. My cousin, Me Me Mockingbird, is a copycat, too. But even he can't do a *whoooo*."

38

"That didn't give you the right to steal Mournful Owl's *whoooo*," said Flatfoot Fox. "You must give it back to him right NOW."

"I don't know what all the fuss is about," Copycat Catbird said. "Fuss, fuss, fuss. I'll give the *whoooo* back. I don't need it anymore. I can do a great *whoooo* now. Listen."

He *whooooed* and *whooooed*.

"It's a great *whoooo*," said Silly Goose, "but Mournful Owl does it better."

Secretary Bird nodded. "Case closed," he said. "But I don't know," he told Flatfoot Fox, "how you knew who the thief was."

Flatfoot Fox didn't answer.

He was already on the way to tell Mournful Owl the wonderful news.

Silly Goose reached Mournful Owl first. As soon as he saw Mournful Owl, he called out, "I found your *whoooo*."

Secretary Bird nipped him. "*You* found it, you silly goose?"

"*We* found it," Silly Goose said. "Copycat Catbird stole it."

"Borrowed, borrowed. I don't steal," said Copycat Catbird. He had flown after them to explain to Mournful Owl.

40

Mournful Owl stared at them with his big, sad eyes.

"Your *whoooo* is in Copycat Catbird's voice box," Flatfoot Fox told Mournful Owl. He turned to Copycat Catbird. "Give it back. NOW!"

"Open wide," said Copycat Catbird.

"Will it hurt?" asked Silly Goose.

Mournful Owl opened his mouth. In popped his *whoooo*. He tried it out.

"*Whoooo. Whoooo.*"

His eyes grew bright and happy.

When Flatfoot Fox and Secretary Bird left, they could hear the sound following them.

"*Whoooo. Whoooo.*"

6
Flatfoot Fox — Always Ready

"Well, that's over," said Secretary Bird.

He and Flatfoot Fox were home again.

"I think this was your most unusual case," said Secretary Bird. Then he looked puzzled. "But I still don't understand how you knew who the thief was."

"It was simple," said Flatfoot Fox.

Secretary Bird waited. It didn't sound simple.

"The woodpecker gave me the clue," said Flatfoot Fox.

"Because he sounded like a frog? How was that a clue?"

"When I heard him imitate a frog, I thought of other birds who did imitations. I thought of Me Me Mockingbird first. But he just imitates other birds'

45

songs. Then I remembered Copycat Catbird. He imitates animals as well."

"Oh," said Secretary Bird. "Of course."

"And I also remembered that Copycat Catbird is always trying to add new sounds."

"So you thought he must have heard Mournful Owl's *whoooo* and wanted to imitate it," said Secretary Bird.

"And I was right." Flatfoot Fox smiled.

"Yes. You were right."

I could have thought of that, Secretary Bird thought. This case really was simple. Well, wait and see, he told himself. Next time he would solve a case. Then he could become the smartest detective in the whole world.

Flatfoot Fox laughed. He seemed to know what Secretary Bird was thinking.

He didn't say a word, however, for his next case arrived in a rush.

"Good," Flatfoot Fox said. "Maybe this next case will be even more interesting."

He was ready.

The smartest detective in the whole world was
always ready.

Also available from Scholastic:

Flatfoot Fox and the Case of the Missing Eye
Flatfoot Fox and the Case of the Nosy Otter